FINAL SLAPSHOT

Jean C. Joachim

Moonlight Books

Dedication

To hockey fans everywhere.

Special Dedication

To Trent McCleary, who inspired this story.

Acknowledgment

A huge thank you to V. L. Locey, who kept the hockey part of this story accurate. Thank you, also, to Jami Davenport, who invited me into the hockey holiday anthology, where this story was first published. Without her generous invitation, this novella would never have been written. Thank you to my editor, Sherri Good, and my proofreader, Renee Waring.

The Final Slapshot

Edited by Sherri Good
Proofread by Renee Waring

PUBLISHER
Moonlight Books

Chapter One

Harry "Deke" Edwards, defenseman for the Hartford Huskies pro hockey team, walked into Jasper's Jewelry on Park Street.

"Can I help you, sir?" the man behind the counter asked.

"Yeah. Diamonds. A bracelet?"

"A tennis bracelet?"

"Naw. Hockey. I play hockey."

"No, I meant the style of bracelet. May I show you?"

"Sure, sure."

Embarrassed and feeling like an idiot, Deke wandered around the store, peering into the cases. He spotted a pair of diamond earrings. He'd get both the bracelet and the earrings. Hell, it was Christmas, wasn't it? Maybe their last one as husband and wife. A heaviness surrounded his heart.

"Here you go, sir," the clerk said.

Deke held up the bracelet, fit it around his thick wrist. Of course, it was too small for him. It should fit his wife, Kitty, just right.

"I'll take it. And those earrings over there, too."

"Yes, sir." The clerk bustled over to the case to extract the baubles. "Shall I wrap them separately?"

"Please."

"As a gift?"

"Christmas gift."

"I'll be right back."

As he looked out the window, Deke shook his head. Was he nuts? Who buys expensive jewelry for his wife right before he meets with his lawyer to discuss divorce? The clerk returned and handed him the presents.

With a tiny, elegant shopping bag in his massive paw, Deke headed for the parking lot. He maneuvered his car down the highway to Monroe. He pulled up in front of a two-story office building. The icy wind penetrated his thin jacket during the short walk from the car.

Deke and Kitty had been living together only part-time for three years. She ran an art gallery in Washington, D.C. while he played for the Huskies in Connecticut. Was it fair to keep her tied to him when she had a life elsewhere? Inheriting the gallery from her aunt three years ago had been their undoing. She wanted to run it, and he wanted to play hockey. They agreed to live apart during the season. Off-season, he trotted down to D.C. to bunk in with her.

He'd found it uncomfortable being "Mr. Kitty" to the folks in her circle. She was too good for him, and he'd always known it. Smart, and sophisticated, she understood all kinds of crap about art. He couldn't distinguish between modern art and a finger painting. Kitty was sweet, hot, gorgeous—and she laughed at his dumb jokes. How could he not fall for her?

By year two, they had patched together a disjointed schedule of meet-ups. Often, during the week, Kitty joined him in hotels on the road, especially when they were in towns close to D.C., like Baltimore and Philly. Their separation made times together intense and hot. Frequently, it was sack time first and catching up second.

When he was in Hartford, the loneliness ate at him. Although they'd speak often, almost every night, he hated going to bed and waking up alone. Distance grew between them. Calling ceased to be regular. Some nights he'd fall asleep before touching base with her and regret it in the morning.

Puck bunnies in faraway towns tempted him, but he resisted. Sex on the road would have been easy—just fuck and leave. He simply refused to jeopardize his eight-year marriage for a roll in the hay. Besides, no easy lay could compare with making love to Kitty.

He opened the door of his lawyer's office and sat down in the waiting area.

"Mr. Cohen will see you now," the receptionist said.

Deke ambled into the tasteful, mahogany-paneled room. He occupied a chair opposite the mammoth wood desk. Herb Cohen talked on the phone. He swiveled to face Deke and gave him a smile. When he hung up, he raised his gaze to Deke's.

"What can I do for you, Harry?"

"I think it's time to give Kitty a divorce."

"Divorce?"

"You remember. We talked about it. Give her half of our assets and the house in Washington, and whatever else she wants. Okay?"

"Shouldn't we talk about this?"

"We did. She deserves to have her freedom, not be stuck with a washed-up hockey player."

"Since when are you washed up?"

Deke waved his hand. "Never mind about that."

"And what about you?"

"Me?" he laughed. "I've had eight years with the most wonderful woman in the world. I'd say I've been more than lucky." Deke pushed to his feet and strode to the door. "Send me the bill."

"Are you sure?"

"About the bill?"

"About the divorce."

"No, but I do lots of things I'm not sure about. It's only right she get her life back before it's too late."

"It's a no-fault state. So this should be easy."

"Good. That means it'll be cheap, too. Right?"

"Maybe. It depends on her."

"She won't fight it."

He exited the building. Once in his car, he felt empty. Something was missing. Oh, yes. He'd left his heart in Herb Cohen's office.

ON THE DRIVE HOME, he remembered their last big fight. It had happened when they were still together full time.

"I'm not ready to have children yet." Kitty had been sitting at her dressing table, brushing her auburn hair.

"Christ, Kitty, want to wait 'til you're forty?"

"That's ridiculous! I'm only twenty-seven. Can't you wait five years?"

"Five years! I could be dead in five years."

"Then we'll freeze your sperm."

"Nobody's freezin' nothing of mine."

"You don't understand."

"I understand you don't wanna have kids with me. You gonna run that stupid art gallery instead?"

"It's not stupid. I just want a chance at a career. Just for a few years."

"A few years? Yeah, right. Why didn't you tell me you didn't want to have kids before we got married?"

"I didn't say that. I just want to wait. Please, Harry?

"I can't force you," he said, turning away from her. "Go be a career woman."

"Thanks."

"Don't thank me. I'm backed into a corner here," he said, anger rising in his chest. He'd stomped out of the bedroom, down the stairs and into his car. He'd driven around for an hour. When he'd returned home, Kitty wasn't there.

Damn it! Why did life have to be so hard? Things had been going great for him. Being the top defenseman on the Huskies and married to the hottest, nicest woman—Deke had captured the brass ring of life. Now, half of that dream had burst into flames. Was there any way to keep the other half from crumbling?

The next morning, after sleeping past his alarm, Deke pushed thoughts about his marriage out of his mind. At nine thirty, he turned his car toward Hartford and headed for the Huskies' arena. He'd be late for morning skate, usually a big deal with Coach Timmons. But Coach had gone soft on Deke, allowing him an infraction or two, pretending not to notice. Deke worried. That couldn't be good.

He parked and hustled into the locker room. He threw on sweats and headed for the exercise room. Warm-ups came first. The other guys were already bending and stretching.

"Glad you could fit us into your schedule, Mr. Edwards," Sonny, the head trainer said.

"Sorry, Sonny. Won't happen again."

The trainer shot him a cold glance and continued leading the men. Deke fell in with the back line.

"What the fuck?" It was Buzzy MacConnell, a winger, and Deke's best friend.

"Stuff," Deke muttered and turned his gaze to the front of the room.

Fifteen minutes later, they headed for the ice. Deke took his time getting his skates on. Feeling a glare, he looked up. Eyes narrowed, Sonny rubbed his chin as he stared. Deke swallowed. The trainer was getting too close. He'd catch on.

Pushing up, Deke joined in with the skate warm-up. He circled the rink, trying to keep up.

A whistle blew. "Faster!" Sonny yelled.

Buzzy caught up to Deke. His brows knitted as he glanced at his buddy.

"You okay?" Buzzy asked.

"Shut the fuck up," Deke growled, increasing his speed.

Sonny took them through passing and shooting drills. Deke and two other defensemen blocked. After an hour, they broke. Deke ripped off his skates in record time and charged into the bathroom. Locking himself in a stall, he whipped out an inhaler and shot two puffs into his lungs. It didn't help. The doctor told him to forget the nebulizer, but Deke insisted on trying it.

He collapsed on the toilet seat and bent over, waiting until his breathing returned to normal. It didn't take long. As soon as he stopped the exertion, his chest calmed down. He shut his eyes tight, his lips clamped together into a fine line as he recalled his last visit to the doctor.

"How long until I can breathe normal again?" Harry asked the doctor.

"This isn't going to get better, Harry."

"That's what you said. But I swear, I was able to go longer yesterday."

"You're fooling yourself. The surgery took out fifteen percent of your windpipe. It's not going to grow back. You can't move as fast as you used to. It's a fact. Try to accept it."

"Accept it? You want me to accept that one injury has taken away my whole life?"

"I'm sorry. I wish I had better news. We had to do that to save your life."

"Yeah? Well some fuckin' life you left me with," Harry muttered, slamming out of the doctor's office.

He'd picked up a bottle of his favorite vodka and gotten blasted that night, all by himself. Sonny had told him exercise does miraculous things. According to him, "Men have made parts of their bodies come back enough to continue playing." Deke refused to accept the doctor's prediction that this was the end of the line for his life on ice. He'd simply have to work harder.

Tomorrow, they'd leave for Washington, to play the Wolverines. Kitty would stay with him—the perfect time to tell her about his plan. She'd never asked for a divorce, but the strain of separation showed in her face. Her phone calls had petered out. Deke had no clue what was going on in her life, yet, she stuck with him.

After the injury, she'd rushed to the hospital and held his hand when he came out of surgery. That one slapshot had changed everything. He had to man up. It was time to put Kitty ahead of himself and set her free to have a better life.

Deke managed to make it through the rest of skate time. He turned down Buzz's invitation to dine with him and his wife to head home, alone, and prepare for the trip. He watched some reels of the Wolverines while he ate. A smile crept across his face. Hell, he found their weak spot within fifteen minutes. Defending against them would be a piece of cake.

Their best shooter was left-handed, making it easier to sneak up on him and block his shot. He chuckled. It didn't look like the guy had good aim, or was it only that game? If he could still defend, Kitty and Sonny wouldn't know the truth—at least not for a while.

He climbed into bed and turned out the light, sinking into a deep sleep. Deke was right there, skating against the Boston Bulldogs. They were hot, the toughest team on the ice. He scrambled to block the forward, heading for the Huskies goal.

There it was, wham! A perfect slapshot at the goal! Deke leaped into the air, sailing across the crease. The puck hit him in the neck, crushing his larynx and windpipe. He crashed down hard. Gasping for breath, he barely managed to skate to the bench, where he collapsed. Everything went dark, until he awoke in the recovery room.

Dreaming, Deke tossed, clutching his throat, the memory of being unable to breathe flashing back. Sweat broke out on his face, soaking his pillow. He jolted awake. Damn, would he ever stop reliving that horrible day?

During his recovery, Kitty commuted to her gallery, spending weekdays with him, but returning to D.C. for weekends, when the gallery did most of it's business. The accident jump-started their marriage. As if on a honeymoon, they couldn't get enough time together. Deke counted the hours until Kitty returned to him.

He figured you didn't need a big windpipe to skate. The injury wasn't like racking up a knee or breaking an ankle. He'd be on the ice again once he recovered from the surgery and regained his strength.

But if you can't breathe, you can't skate. Or at least skate fast enough to play pro hockey. For the first time, he'd been dumped on the disabled list. After a month, the Huskies brought Deke back. They'd kept an eye on him but hadn't started him yet. Grateful to hide his breathing condition longer, Deke didn't complain. On this trip, Coach Timmons told Deke he'd start.

He'd been all for it, until morning skate. Sure, the doc had told him the truth, but he didn't believe it. Doing breathing exercises at home should bring his wind back. But not so far. Punching his pillows and rearranging the sheet and blanket, he changed position. How much longer could he pretend?

KITTY PUT DOWN THE phone. The doctor confirmed her worst fear—Harry's career was over. Her stomach turned over and her eyes wetted. Harry, her strong, handsome, powerful husband reduced to a has-been. How could this be? Just a little reduction in the windpipe and—blam!—game over.

Blotting her cheeks with a tissue, she swallowed. Her hands fisted as the word *unfair* breezed through her brain. He'd turned himself into a pretzel with insane travel, a D.C. home, and other expenses, supporting her career. The gallery was doing great, even with the crazy schedule she kept. When Kitty flew off to join Harry, Donna, her assistant, took over. Success knocked at Kitty's door, and now, Harry, a proud man, would be kissing fame goodbye.

Anxiety clutched her gut. How would their marriage survive? The tipping of the delicate scale would require new ways to cope. Now, he could be with her fulltime in Washington. But would he want that? Harry move into her digs and be in her shadow? Never.

Her heart squeezed. This couldn't be the end of Kitty and Harry. She padded to the kitchen and put up a fresh pot of coffee. It was nine, but she had no appetite for breakfast. There had to be a way to reorganize their life so that their marriage would survive.

After adding milk and sugar to her mug, she dialed her mother. At the sound of her voice, Kitty burst into tears. Unable to stop crying, she couldn't speak.

"What's wrong? Kitty? Dear? Please. Tell me what's wrong."

Kitty took a deep breath and brought her phone to her ear. "Mom?"

"Kitty? What's happened?"

"Mom. It's awful. It's terrible. Harry's career is over, and he won't tell me and he won't stop playing and it's terrible. I don't know what's going to happen," she said, stringing the words together.

"What are you talking about?"

Kitty explained what the doctor said.

"I'm so sorry to hear that, dear. I'm sure you two can work something out."

"You don't know Harry. He's so proud. He wants to be the breadwinner, the man, you know?"

"Oh, yes, I do. Your father's the same way. Still, if he can't do that, then you two must find something else."

"If he keeps playing, he might get hurt again. Worse this time," Kitty said, biting her lip.

"Let me think, talk to your father. I'll call you back tonight."

"Okay."

Kitty hit the shower and got dressed. The gallery didn't open until noon, but she had a ton of things to do. Harry'd be coming down and they'd be together. This trip, she'd go to his game. She needed to see him in action. After all, it might be his last time. She shivered at the thought, picked up her briefcase and headed for the street.

As she walked, she stopped to watch Macy's eye-catching Christmas window displays. Christmas shopping! That would brighten her mood. This year, she'd be buying Harry gifts with her own money, bucks she'd made at the gallery. A smile spread across her face. Maybe it was time Harry got used to her carrying more of the load.

The store boasted garlands with shiny silver and blue balls, Christmas trees decorated in gold and red ornaments, or Christmas plaid. Each department showcased a different tree color combination. Kitty made a note to buy a tree and two wreaths for the house in West Hartford. She'd make the purchase online and have the decorations shipped.

She stopped first in menswear. Harry needed new shirts. Maybe flannel this year. If he didn't have to dress in suits and ties anymore, he didn't need more dress shirts. The image of her tall man in a plaid flannel shirt gave her gooseflesh. Her fingers tingled as she imagined pressing them against his chest, strong under the soft cotton.

Perhaps there would be some perks to his not playing hockey? For example, days spent in bed, talking about what he should do next. A shiver ran up her spine, bringing heat to other places.

"Can I help you?" asked a salesman.

"Yes. Flannel shirts, extra-large?"

"Right this way."

Kitty perused the selection.

"I'll take the red plaid. He has dark hair and eyes."

"Good choice. Black Watch goes with all coloring," the salesman said.

"Oh, yes. I like that one. I'll take it, too."

"Wrap as a gift?"

"Please. Christmas paper?"

"Of course. Anything else?"

"Bathrobes?"

"Right his way."

Kitty hummed *Jingle Bells* as she followed the man. If she couldn't fix what was wrong with Harry, at least she could buy him gifts to let him know she'd been thinking of him. Love swelled in her heart as she made her way through the store, racking up a bill of more than five hundred dollars. Nothing was too good for her man.

The salesman took the items and sent them to be shipped. They'd arrive before Kitty. Perfect. She sighed. This Christmas had to be special. Who knew where they'd be next year?

Chapter Two

The way his sweat glands worked overtime, you'd think he faced the last game in the Stanley Cup playoffs. Deke had faked his way through morning skate, again. Not that he'd fooled the trainers or his coach. He noticed their narrowed eyes following him as he sprinted across the ice. After half an hour, he huffed and puffed, bent over in a corner to catch his breath.

He couldn't continue to stall or say he needed a few more weeks. The Huskies were losing. They needed Deke in top form now.

"You're starting in D.C.," Coach had said a week ago.

It was do or die time. Deke stocked up on inhalers and prayers. Harry "Deke" Edwards was all about pro hockey. He figured with Kitty's success with her gallery, she'd probably dump him if he got put out to pasture. He'd have nothing. The thought kicked up his heart rate.

He packed with care, bringing his new aftershave, *Secret Desire*. His secret desire had nothing to do with sex. Every night he prayed his windpipe would stretch by fifteen percent. Still, the cologne smelled great. Kitty'd notice he'd switched brands.

Kitty! His mind turned to his luscious wife. God, he could hardly wait to get her alone. He needed sex, love, and laughter—and she'd supply all three. He sat back in his comfortable seat on the private Husky jet and closed his eyes. Sleep would wipe away his concerns, as long as he didn't have that nightmare. Fuck. If that horrible dream returned while he was asleep in the air, he'd be humiliated. Still, exhaustion prevailed, and his eyes drifted shut.

Next thing he knew, the plane touched down. They boarded a bus to the posh hotel in Washington, down the block from the Capital One Arena. The men piled out. Deke texted the address to Kitty and lugged his small duffle into the lobby. His phone dinged as he rode the elevator up to the fifth floor. His wife would be there in half an hour.

On the road, the team met for dinner, then they had the evening to themselves. The married players with spouses bunking in didn't have to attend. They were on their own. In his room, Deke dumped his bag on a stand, grabbed the hotel's menu and stretched out on the bed.

Steak, prime rib, baked stuffed shrimp—the selections made his mouth water. After making love, they could head downstairs for a great meal, then spend the rest of the evening in bed. Deke wouldn't tell Kitty about his trip to the lawyer's office. She'd find out soon enough. He wanted as much time with her as he could get before her love turned to hate. Isn't that what happened during divorce? Didn't couples who once couldn't get enough of each other wish they had a license to kill? He'd read about it on the Internet. He'd never hate Kitty, no matter what she did. Someday, she'd understand he did it for her.

Tomorrow's game was do or die. He had to perform. Maybe not up to his old standard, but close. The team counted on him. Deke drew out the five inhalers he'd packed. He kissed each one.

"Make it happen," he said, before stuffing them away so Kitty wouldn't see.

Not telling her about his breathing problem or his conversation with the doctor meant she'd still love him, think of him as her hero. How could he admit that he wasn't the man he used to be? Sure, she'd profess her love anyway, and all that shit, but their relationship would never be the same. Deke wouldn't be the invincible guy she'd married, the man who could defeat any forward, solve any problem, and keep her screaming in the sack.

She hadn't signed up to be hitched to a thirty-three-year-old has-been. He had to come across on the ice. He showered, shaved, slapped on *Secret Desire,* and checked his watch. A knock on the door brought a smile to his face. Right on time! He opened it, and his wife stepped in. She wore a stunning, forest green, wrap-around wool coat.

She leaned back against the door and slowly pulled on the sash. The garment fell away, revealing her slender body clad only in thigh-high black stockings, black bikini panties, and a lace teddy.

"Ho, ho, ho, Harry. Merry Christmas."

He laughed and pulled her into his arms.

LYING NEXT TO HIS WIFE, he asked, "It's seven. Dinner?"

"Just a few more minutes?"

She snuggled her naked self into his body, snaking her arms around his middle, resting her cheek on his hairy chest. She took a deep breath. His masculine scent mixed with that new cologne pleased her. She kissed his chest. "That was great."

"You're amazing, Kitty. I swear you have the heart of a hooker."

"A hooker?" She bolted upright.

"I didn't mean it that way. I meant that you know how to please a guy, to do it right."

"Oh?" She cocked an eyebrow at him. "And what do you know about how a hooker has sex?"

His face reddened. "I was young. Only once. The guys. You know. Initiation, sort of."

"Oh, I see. Better have been before you met me."'

"Before? Oh, way before, *waaayy* before! Trust me. Once we got together, who'd need a hooker?"

Her frown deepened. "Well, thanks a lot!" She jumped out of bed and opened her suitcase.

Harry followed her. "No, no. I didn't mean it like that. I meant that you're so amazing in the sack, who could ever want or need anyone else?"

She stopped, turned, and glared at him.

"You know I always put my foot in it. I'm sorry. I just meant that you're an incredible lover. So responsive. That's all. Please, Kitty." He reached for her hand.

She allowed him to ease her back to bed.

"Where were we?" he asked, lying down and lifting her with his massive hands to nestle beside him.

She snuggled closer, listening to his heart. The beat was as strong as ever. Her fingertips pressed slightly into his muscles. *Why can't his lungs be stronger, his windpipe stretch back to normal?* She sighed. He must have a reason for not telling her the truth, so she kept her knowledge to herself.

"Hungry?" he asked, plucking the menu off the nightstand.

Only for you. "Sure."

"The restaurant here looks pretty good. Wanna try it?"

"Okay. Quick meal, then back here?"

"Of course. We're just getting started," he replied.

"Hmm. Just the appetizer. We have the main course yet to come," she said.

"It's been a while."

"Too long. Last one dressed is a rotten egg," she said, leaping out of bed and attacking her small suitcase.

"Last one dressed, gives first blow job," he countered.

She bent over laughing. Harry chuckled and raced into his clothes, finishing first. He backed her onto the bed.

"Or we could have food sent up," he said, his voice low.

"We could," she replied, pulling his head down, meeting his lips with hers. Harry pushed up on the bed, looming over her.

"I love you, Harry," she whispered, her eyes wet.

"I love you back. What's the matter?" His brows knitted, his lips compressed into a frown.

"Nothing. Just tears of joy. Happy to be with you," she lied.

He cocked an eyebrow. He'd often called her a bad liar, and he'd been right. But she had to keep up the pretense, as long as he did, anyway.

He captured her legs between his and lowered his mouth to her breast. "I'm having my first course right here."

Kitty giggled, slipping her arms around his neck. Harry sat up.

"Okay, okay. That'll have to wait. Let's eat." He pushed up off the bed and offered her his hand. She took it and dressed quickly. It didn't matter what she wore, because as soon as the meal was over, she'd be taking it off.

When they were decent, they walked hand-in-hand down the hall to the elevator. In the dining room, Harry slipped a twenty to the maître d' and requested a secluded table. They settled in, ordered shrimp cocktail, prime rib for Harry and crab cakes for Kitty.

He laced their fingers. "This is a big game. The Wolverines are better this year."

"Are you starting?"

"Yep. Coach said I looked good enough to give it a go. We'll see."

Her heart leaped into her throat. This was Harry's trial. Tomorrow's game would tell the tale. Her nerves kicked up. She'd have to keep him occupied, give him something besides the game to think about. Kitty smiled to herself. Easy, peasy—in the bedroom, the man was putty in her hands.

Stuck for a reply, Kitty cast a grateful glance at the waiter, who arrived with their food. She threw out a bit about the gallery and a new exhibit she planned for spring. Anything to distract him and avoid fessing up that she knew the truth about his condition.

As they finished up dessert, Kitty slipped her foot out of her pump and ran it up and down Harry's shin. His head snapped up. He stared straight at her.

"Startin' something?" he asked. A slight redness crept up his neck.

"Maybe instead of coffee?" she asked, raising her eyebrows.

Harry shot her a grin and motioned for the waiter. "Check, please."

SUITING UP IN THE LOCKER room, Deke put his "lucky" inhaler in his pocket. After he dressed, he took four puffs, twice the recommended dosage. He didn't give a shit about side effects, he needed his air passages open all the way.

He took a deep breath but didn't notice any difference. He threw the inhaler against the wall, breaking the plastic holder.

"Fuckin' thing! No damn good."

"Easy, Deke. Easy," Buzzy said.

After he dumped the broken device in the garbage and folded a new one into his hand, he headed for the rink with his teammates. Would this be his last time? He glanced across the ice at the Wolverines. Young, restless, and ready to beat the balls off the Huskies. Pumped to keep those bastards away from the goal, Deke smiled as the adrenaline flowed. He itched to smash a forward into the boards.

"Ready?" Coach Timmons asked him.

He nodded. The knitted eyebrows on Timmons' face relaxed a bit. He patted Deke on the shoulder. Skating out on the ice for the national anthem, he made eye contact with Kitty. God, he wished she hadn't come. He did everything he could to talk her out of it. If he was going down in flames, did it have to be in front of the woman he loved? Shit. He took his position.

The whistle blew. The Huskies won the face-off. Deke backed up, keeping alert. The puck was Buzz's. He zoomed up the ice, heading for the Wolverine goal. Checked, he managed to get a quick pass off to another forward before the Wolverine shoved him into the boards.

The slippery little puck zigzagged back and forth between both teams, never staying in either team's possession long enough to get knocked across a goal line. Evenly matched, the Wolverines and Huskies scrambled for control. When necessary, Deke dropped back and got his stick on the puck twice, sending it zooming to a forward.

By the third period, with no score, both teams snorted in frustration. Energy mixed with testosterone, thickening the air. Deke narrowed his eyes as two Wolverine forwards stared at him and whispered. Shit, they pegged him as the weak link. He'd been able to cover, with help from his teammates, but with his breath short, he'd never survive double-teaming.

The two men made a mad dash at the goal. Deke took off skating past the crease. They came full force and plowed into him, knocking him down. He jumped up and took off after them.

"Hey, Grandma, can't catch me."

"Pussy!"

Deke saw red and charged. His lungs screamed, but when they sped past him, he pushed ahead, racing for the puck. Gulping air and gasping for breath, he slowed but kept moving. They breezed by, taunting him. His legs leaden, he reached for the puck but missed. Still, Deke chased his tormentors. Then it happened. Everything went black. He dropped on the ice in a dead faint.

He opened his eyes to stare into the worried blues of Sonny, who held an oxygen mask to his nose. As he lay there, air returned to his lungs. The scoreboard showed a goal for the Wolverines. Those assholes had put one in the net before he passed out.

"That's it, Deke. You're out," the trainer said.

"Says who?"

"Coach, that's who."

Buzzy offered a hand and as Deke rose, a cheer went up from the crowd. One glance at the stands and he saw Kitty on her feet. This was it. He was through, finished. Taken out forever by a slapshot to the neck three months ago.

Tears stung at the backs of his eyes. He hit the locker room and fired the other four inhalers against the wall, finding little satisfaction in the sound of shattering plastic. Done. Finished. Put out to pasture. Has-been. There must be fifty words for what he'd become—none of them good.

The trainer returned with more oxygen, but Deke waved him away. Deke? Deke no more, just plain old Harry now. He plopped down on a bench and disrobed. The doctor's words rang in his ears.

"You don't grow back part of your windpipe, Harry. It won't stretch back to its former size, either. It's just not happening."

Harry put his pads and skates in his locker. Sonny approached.

"Coach wants to see you after the game."

Harry nodded. He took a shower and dressed in street clothes before returning to the team box. Once he donned his suit and tie, he could no longer warm the bench. Pain seared through him as he watched another defenseman allow a second goal for D.C. The final whistle blew. Wolverines two, Huskies zero.

Humiliation burned in his chest, but he had to face his teammates. He entered the locker room last.

"Hey, how you doin'?" Buzzy asked.

The rest of the team echoed his concern. They stopped what they were doing and turned their attention to Harry.

"I'm okay. Okay for life. But not for hockey."

"That was a fluke though, right?" the team captain asked.

Harry shook his head. "No. I wish."

"But you've been working out with us?"

"Yeah. And gasping for breath for fifteen minutes after each session. Nope. The surgeon had to take fifteen percent of my windpipe out to save my life. I'll never have the stamina I once had. Hockey is over for me."

A chorus of boos and sympathetic comments warmed him. Coach stuck his head in and motioned to Harry. He nodded. *Here it comes—the axe.* The hallway leading to the coach seemed like a ten-mile trek.

"Come in, Deke," Coach Timmons said, motioning to a chair.

Harry eased down.

"We gave you every chance to come back, even though the doctor said it wasn't likely you'd be able to play like you used to. He said your speed would be off. But we wanted to try, give you a shot. Today proved the doctor right. You're off the roster, Deke. I'm sorry, but I have no choice. We've talked about where else we could use you. We can offer you a job as a scout, if you want to stay with the club. Of course, we'll buy out your contract, then put you on as an employee. Think about it. Talk it over with your wife."

Coach Timmons stood up.

"Thanks, Coach," Harry said, rising.

They shook hands and Harry left the barn. Did it take him an hour to hit the parking lot? Or did it only seem like walking underwater? Shock slowed everything. Tears pricked at the backs of his eyes, but he blinked them away. What would he say to Kitty, waiting in the car?

WASHINGTON, D.C.

Kitty stood at her townhouse window, gazing at the moon and frowning. Their last conversation before he left with the team came to mind. He'd fessed up about his injury, then roared about the unfairness of it. She let him. After all, he deserved time to yell, scream, and stomp around—get it out of his system. But instead, after his initial reaction, he crumbled like stale bread.

She'd seen Harry's anger before. Kitty could deal with anger, outrage, fury—but not sadness, not this deflated, silent Harry who sat before her, head in his hands. Fear spiked up her spine. Harry had always been the fixer, but how could he fix this? He was broken, and she had to help him. Was she up to the task? If she loved him, she'd find a way.

Her brows knit as she considered the solution put forth by the Huskies. Some offer—become a scout. That involved more traveling than playing on the team. And he'd be removed from hockey, always the observer, never a participant.

Her eyes clouded, then watered. Harry on the road all the time would finish them. Grabbing a tissue, she dabbed at her eyes and blew her nose. There had to be something else that could bring them together. She sighed and returned to the bedroom to finish packing. Tomorrow was Christmas Eve, and Christmas spirit had flown the coop.

"Merry Christmas, Harry, you're fired. Out with the trash. Yeah, we needed you defending our goal, but now that you're slower than a camel, you're gone," she muttered to herself, her tone bitter. "Oh, by the way, we'll throw an old dog like you a bone. Scout for us, for one-tenth of what you were making before. And one hundred percent more travel."

She slammed the top down on her suitcase and typed "National Airport" in on her Uber app and headed for the front door. Slipping on the mink coat Harry gave her for their third Christmas, she trudged down the stairs of their townhouse to the foyer.

Lying on the floor was the mail. She stooped to pick it up. An envelope with her name on it accompanied an assortment of Christmas cards. She checked the return address.

"Hmm. H. Cohen, Attorney-at-Law. Probably just junk mail. Guy looking to do a will or something," she said. The honking of a horn drew her attention. No time to throw that letter out, so she stuffed it in her purse and rushed outside to the Uber cab waiting by the sidewalk.

The airport was stuffed to overflowing. Kitty chided herself for flying when she could have taken a train.

"Trains are crowded during the holidays, too. People sneeze in your face. And it takes fuckin' forever," Harry had said. "Fly. Go first class."

"It's a waste of money on such a short flight."

"I don't care. It's Christmas. I want you to arrive happy."

"I'll be spending it with you. Why wouldn't I be happy?" she'd asked, snaking her arms around his middle.

He'd kissed her. "First class, Kit."

"Okay."

Silently, she thanked him. He'd been right. Harry looked out for her 24/7. He took care of her with the same zeal that he defended the Husky net—all in.

Once she'd squeezed through the line of bodies waiting to board their flights, she sank into a roomy, comfortable seat and sipped champagne. Staring out the window at the lights of D.C., her mind turned to Christmas. Every year, her family and their friends dropped in for a catered Christmas Eve buffet at their spacious home in West Hartford.

Christmas Day, her favorite day of the year, belonged to Kitty and Harry alone, since he only had three days off. She loved Christmas Day. They'd start off by making love, then have a leisurely breakfast that stretched into lunch. They'd open their gifts, watch movies, then make love again. Kitty'd patch together a meal using leftovers from the night before.

But this year? How would they get through it? Emotion welled up inside her. She fished in her bag for a tissue. There was that stupid letter.

"Miss, can you toss this for me, please?"

The stewardess took the envelope. She looked it over. "Are you sure. It looks like a personal letter."

Kitty took it back and studied it. The woman had been correct, it didn't have any of the usual stuff of direct mail on the envelope. Hmm, a lawyer letter, just what she needed. Downing the last of her drink, she ripped open the envelope and read the contents.

HARRY GOT IN HIS CAR at the arena and drove to his home in West Hartford. They lived in a beautiful house, roomy, and decorated with taste and class by Kitty. Harry spent most of his days in the great room. With two sectional sofas, a huge stone fireplace, giant plasma television, and long dining table, it served all his needs, except sleeping.

The entire trip home, Harry focused on the Husky's offer of a scouting job. It wouldn't pay much, not in comparison to his multi-million-dollar contract as a top defenseman. He'd be on the road at least nine months of the year. With the divorce in the works, maybe the scouting job would work. He'd travel too much to keep their marriage together. Hell, it would be a good excuse to give Kitty her freedom. Sure beat admitting he'd failed as a husband.

Harry had asked Timmons for time to consider the offer. He'd take the buyout and split it with Kitty. Then she'd have the financial support she needed to take the gallery to the next level. Kitty amazed him with her willingness to work hard and find a way to make an art gallery profitable enough to keep going. The last thing she needed was a has-been like him, tagging along, dragging her down.

Alice, their housekeeper, had seen to it the snow on the front walk had been cleared. Harry put his key in the lock and entered. The scent of fresh pine greeted him. He put down his bag, ambled over to the bar and poured a Chivas on the rocks. Then he flipped on a Christmas CD Kitty had made with their favorite songs.

His housekeeper had put up the two wreaths Kitty had sent, and the Christmas tree stood in a place of honor, waiting to be decorated. He sighed. This year, he'd have all the time in the world to dress the tree.

A fire had been laid. He lit a piece of newspaper and held it up the chimney to create a draft, then shoved it under the logs. He toed off his shoes and sat down on the sofa, watching the fire.

The crackle of the dry wood added to the atmosphere. Climbing the stairs to the bedroom, he rummaged through his drawer until his fingers found Kitty's Christmas gifts. He padded downstairs and put the two small boxes under the tree.

Reaching under the sofa, he pulled out a large one. Inside was the down comforter she'd coveted at the specialty shop in town. He placed that next to the more expensive gifts. Harry made his way around the room, remembering where he'd stashed each present he'd accumulated during the year. There was the coffee table book with huge color pictures of the work of her favorite artists. And the purse she'd admired but refused to buy because it was too expensive. Playing Santa Claus to his wife suited Harry.

Once he had all the loot assembled, he poured another drink and hummed along with *Silver Bells,* sung by Nat King Cole. Christmas was set. All he needed was Kitty. He stood by the picture window and watched a soft snowfall. Flakes drifted down, taking their time as if waiting for the perfect spot to land. They coated dark, bare tree limbs on one side, shading them, giving them depth. Stars twinkled like tiny Christmas lights in the sky.

The crunch of tires on the packed snow in the driveway grabbed his attention. He pulled the curtain aside. A limousine parked by the front door. The driver opened the trunk and deposited Kitty's bags by the front stoop. She tipped him, unnecessary because a tip was included, and he doffed his cap.

Swathed in mink up to her chin, his stunning wife marched up the steps, bags in hand. Harry opened the door.

"Kitty! Baby! Merry Christmas!" he said, opening his arms and mustering all the holiday cheer he could.

She stepped closer and slapped him across the face. "Don't you Merry Christmas me!"

Chapter Three

Harry retreated a step. "What the hell?"

"Exactly! What the hell is this?" she asked, waving a folded piece of paper in front of his face.

"I don't know. What is it?"

"A divorce! You want a divorce? Since when? And were you ever going to discuss this with me?" she said, advancing into the room.

Harry backed up.

Kitty slammed the door and made a beeline for the sofa. She rifled pillow after pillow at him. Harry raised his arms, protecting himself.

"You are the lowest form of life on Earth, Harry Edwards! Divorce? How about a funeral, instead? I can arrange that."

Harry picked up the paper from the floor and unfolded it. "Shit."

"Shit? Shit? That's all you have to say?" Tears clouded her eyes as she sank down on the sofa.

"I had no idea Herb was going to do this."

"But you know about it? You want a divorce?"

"No, well, yes. But not really."

"Which it is, Harry?"

"I want to give you your freedom."

"What?" she asked, pushing to her feet.

"And anything else you want."

"Did I ask you for this?"

"No. Figured you wouldn't. But I knew the end of my career was coming. Why should you be tied to some has-been, wash-out? You deserve the best. Your career is skyrocketing. Mine is over. I don't want to hold you back."

When she approached him, he stepped back, rubbing his cheek.

"I'm not going to slap you again. Who do you think you are making decisions like this for me? Since when do I need you to decide what's best for me? If I want a divorce, I'll bloody well tell you myself."

"I knew you'd say that."

Her face reddened. "Why you condescending jerk!"

Risking another assault by his wife, Harry took her upper arm. "Look. I know you're not a cut-and-run person. I get that. It's one of the thousand reasons I married you. But this, this is different. I don't know where I'm going to end up."

"Are you taking the scouting job?"

"I've been considering it. If we weren't married, then being on the road 24/7 works."

He stepped closer. Kitty's gaze searched his face.

"Weren't you going to discuss this with me?"

He shook his head. "I thought about it. But I know you'd want to keep things the same. Kitty, I'm not the same man you married. My life is going to change. I can't tie you to me through this."

"Oh, I see. And for better or worse means nothing?"

He chuckled. "Leave it to you to quote that."

She took off her coat and hung it in the closet, then faced him.

"I get it. Your nice, little perfect life isn't so perfect anymore. You've been thrown a curve. Sorry, wrong sport. Just like everyone else out there. You've been handed something horrible, a twist, a hideous outcome beyond your control. And what do you do? Pull together with me to find a way to change our lives to deal with this? No. You run away. And dump me in the process."

"If you put it like that—"

"What other way is there to put it? If that's what you want to do, then, yes, you're right. You're not the man I married anymore. I married a fighter. Not a wimp who crawls away, tail between his legs, at the first sign of adversity. I'm going upstairs."

She picked up her bag.

"Wait!"

"Why? You've made up your mind. You've given up. I had an idea, but I can see it's too late. So go ahead. Do whatever you want. I'm tired. I'm going to bed."

"No, don't."

She turned her back to him and climbed to the second floor.

Harry rubbed his scruffy face. What had he done? Damn that fucking Herb. Why did he send that letter? If Harry had known, he would have discussed it with Kitty first. Now the whole thing, their relationship—the marriage, had been blown apart. Was he wrong to love her enough to let her go? She didn't see it that way. Could he salvage things, and what was her plan, anyway?

Right from the start, he got that she was way smarter than he. Had he destroyed his marriage by being a stupid idiot? He hoped not. Harry went to the bar, mixed two toddies, then headed for the kitchen. He nuked them and made his way to the bedroom.

WHEN HE OPENED THE door, light from the hall shadowed the figure of someone lying in the massive king-sized bed. Kitty looked so tiny, huddled under a fluffy comforter against the cold. When he entered the room, she didn't budge. She'd done that before—ignored him. He picked up on her level of anger. He balanced the drink tray on the nightstand and flipped on the lamp.

"Hot toddy?"

No response from the little lump.

"Come on. Join me. Get rid of some of that cold in your bones."

Still no response. He sighed.

"Okay, okay. Yes, I talked to a lawyer. He wasn't supposed to send you that letter. I had no idea he'd do that. I just wanted him to get an offer ready. Then I planned to talk to you."

"The lawyer's a prick," came a small voice from under the covers.

"A dumb prick," Harry said.

He took a sip. "This is the best hot toddy I've ever made. Come out, Kitty. I'm sorry. I was wrong. You're right. I never should have done anything without talking to you first."

That did it. Slowly the covers receded, and his beautiful wife's tearstained face emerged.

"Oh, baby. I made you cry? I'm so sorry," he said, reaching for her.

She stiff-armed him and took her glass off the tray. "Don't touch me," she said, before taking a sip.

He frowned at her words and the tone of her voice. This would be no easy fix. He took another sip as his brain maneuvered.

"What was your plan?" he asked.

She simply glared at him and drank.

"Come on. Tell me. I'm sure it's better than mine."

"Anything is better than yours, except death."

He chuckled.

"That wasn't supposed to be funny," she retorted.

"I know, I know. But it was. Look, what do I have to do to get you to talk to me?"

"Say the divorce was the dumbest idea in the world and that you'd never want one."

"Okay. The divorce was the dumbest idea in the world and I'd never want one."

"That's a beginning," she replied.

"What else can I do?"

"Maybe a public flogging?" she asked, arching an eyebrow.

At that, Harry cracked up. A smile played at Kitty's lips. She took a swig and sat back, pulling the covers up to her cover her breasts.

"Do you have to cover up like that?" Harry asked.

"Sex will not get you where you want to go. So back off."

He raised his palms. "Okay. Sorry. Can't help looking."

"Look, just shut up about it. This is serious. Do you know how hard that plane ride was?"

"You read this on the plane?"

"Yes," she said, her voice quivering, her eyes wet.

"Oh my God. I'm so, so sorry."

"I thought you didn't love me anymore and wanted a divorce. I thought you'd met someone on the road and decided to dump me." As she spoke a few tears trickled down her cheeks.

As he brushed the tears away with his thumb, he spoke. "I could never love anyone, want anyone, but you. You have to believe that."

"I used to."

"Oh, baby. God. This is terrible. I didn't mean to hurt you."

"But you did. And then I got angry. I'm celibate all the weeks we're separated and you're fucking around? It drove me crazy. I imagined all kinds of things."

He cupped her cheek and kissed her forehead. "Nope. Been faithful the whole time."

"I wanted to kill you." She wiped her face with a tissue and blew her nose.

"I can imagine. And now?"

"Maybe just beat you up a little."

"Have at me," he said, working to keep away a smile.

She inched nearer and pounded on his chest a couple of times. He didn't flinch.

"There. That make you feel better?" he asked.

"A little. Didn't even bruise you, did I?"

He shook his head, then closed his hand over her little fist. "These are loving hands. Couldn't hurt a fly." He kissed them.

Her eyes filled again. "You shit. You always do something, say something that makes me forgive you."

"That's the idea. I love you, Kitty. Always have. Always will."

"No divorce?" she asked, raising her eyebrows.

"No divorce."

"Good. I love you, too. Harry. We'll figure this out. You'll see."

He rose from the bed, downed the last of his drink, and pulled his sweater over his head. When he got down to his boxers, he crawled into bed.

"What's your plan?" he asked, taking his wife into his arms.

Kitty snuggled down, resting her cheek on his chest.

"Keep an open mind. It's just a jumping off point."

"I'm listening."

"Remember those kids you wanted me to have three years ago?"

"Yeah?"

"I thought we could have them now."

"Really?" His eyebrows shot up.

"Yes. And since you're sort of not working. You're not going to take the scouting job, are you?"

"Not if you don't want me to."

"I don't. I've had enough of being apart all the time. So, anyway. You could be home with the kids."

"Househusband?"

"Stay-at-home dad?"

"Me? Star defenseman of the Huskies? Changing diapers and burping babies?" His eyebrows shot up.

"Your babies. And teaching them to play hockey. You'd be a wonderful dad. Just while I'm working. When I get home, I'll take over."

"And I suppose you want me to cook dinner, too?"

"That would be up to you."

"You've got to be kidding."

"I thought you wanted kids? Hell, three years ago you gave me all kinds of crap for wanting to wait. Now we've waited."

"This is crazy." He shook his head.

"You'll be a great father. You have so much to teach children," she said.

"This is nuts."

"You said that already. Will you at least consider it?"

He frowned, his brow wrinkled.

"Please. Just think about it. You don't have to decide now."

"Okay. I'll think about it."

She shot him a flirtatious glance. "We could work on making the first one now."

A grin lit up his face. "We could. Yes. I'd be up for that."

"You'd have to be up for it to work," she chuckled, sliding the comforter down.

CHRISTMAS EVE DAY

Harry woke up first. He stretched in bed and yawned. It killed him that he felt fine but still couldn't play. It's not like he had a broken limb or was paralyzed, or anything like that. Still a perfect physical specimen plus a scar from the surgery, yet without the stamina to play hockey.

Shaking his head, he hit the john, brushed his teeth, and pushed the frustration out of his mind. Kitty had begged him not to cancel their big party today, and he'd agreed. Harry'd pretend to be happy, cheerful, laughing, and feeling the spirit. No more difficult task could have befallen him.

His wife slept. Her auburn hair complemented the ivory pillowcase. One bare shoulder protruded from the fluffy comforter.

Her skin, smooth, the color of porcelain, tempted him. According to tradition, making love was on the agenda.

After checking his armpits, he eased back into bed. Harry snaked his arm around Kitty's middle. She stirred.

"What time is it?"

"Time for lovin'," he replied.

With a soft chuckle, she rolled over to face him. "Bathroom first."

"Go," he said, giving her rump a squeeze as she flung off the covers.

Hippity-hopping across the cold floor, her bare skin pebbled as she wrapped her arms around her chest. Harry dialed up the temperature on the mattress pad. Within minutes the bathroom door opened, and his beautiful, naked lady scooted across the room and took a flying leap into bed. Harry drew her close, into his warmth.

"Oh, God. It's cold," she said, her teeth chattering a bit.

"Let me warm you up," he snickered.

Kitty wound her leg around his hips and snuggled her face into his neck. A faint, sweet, familiar scent pleased his nose. His hands rubbed up and down the tender skin of her back.

"Warming up?"

She nodded.

Harry loosened his grip so he could reach around in front where luscious breasts flattened against his chest. Blood pumped to his dick as he caressed her body. Kitty kissed him, unleashing his desire. He cupped her rear, pushing her hips to his. Her perfect butt filled his hand. She ran her instep up and down his shin. When her knee moved up, he clasped her thigh, his fingers on the back. He slid them up to her core, grinning as she let out a small gasp.

"Harry," she breathed in his ear.

"Love you," he said.

Kitty wrapped her fingers around his erection while he rubbed her. Then he slid a finger between her folds and inside. She squeezed her eyes shut and stopped moving.

"Damn. You do it. You do it to me. Every time."

"Ready?" he asked.

"Hell, yes."

He mounted her, lubricated himself with her juices, then entered. He loved the feel of her tightness surrounding him. Her moans and movement spiked his desire. At least he could still give his wife pleasure. Gratitude filled his heart. He pumped his hips, his eyes slitted to watch her reaction.

Kitty's face softened, then her eyes squeezed tight as her groans grew louder. She was close. Harry smiled as he watched her give in to an orgasm. He bowed his head, kissing her neck. Sweat broke out on his forehead.

Pushing up on his hands, he stared down at her. Her eyes fluttered open, the green more brilliant.

"Harry," she sighed.

He grinned. "Good one?"

"The best."

Her muscles contracted around him again, spiking his body heat. He increased his pace and closed his eyes as his release took over his body. His balls tightened, one shudder, a hard thrust, and he stopped. Warmth and pleasure coursed through his veins all the way to his toes.

Bracing himself, he lowered his lips to her peak once more, then withdrew. Sitting back on his haunches, his gaze caressed his wife. Beautiful, vulnerable, and satisfied, Kitty smiled at him and combed her fingers through his hair.

"I love you, Harry Edwards."

"And I love you, beautiful."

He fell back on the pillows next to her. Kitty crawled into his embrace, snuggling her head against his shoulder. Harry ran his fingertips over her bare skin. His thoughts returned to his situation, bringing a frown.

"Are you fretting about hockey?" she asked.

"Sort of."

"Forget it. We have the party tonight. There's so much to do. The caterers will be here at noon," she said.

"Noon? It thought it was tonight."

"Tonight, on Christmas Eve, starts at four o'clock. It's an open house. I expect we'll have people coming and going from four until eleven."

"Geez."

"I know. But you always have fun. Tomorrow's our bathrobe-and-leftovers day."

He grinned. "That's the best present of all." This time, he wouldn't be playing, so it didn't matter if he drank or was rested or had exercised during those days off, did it?

"You're a regular party animal, Harry."

He laughed. "Not exactly. What time is it?"

"Ten. Already," she groaned, rolling over on her back.

"Better get dressed before the troops arrive," he muttered, throwing back the covers and swinging his legs over the side.

Kitty grabbed his hand, and, drawing it to her lips, muttered, "Thank you."

Harry bent down, cupped her cheek, and brushed her lips with his. Then he stood and wandered into the bathroom and turned on the shower.

BY ELEVEN THIRTY, HIS house was filled with hot-and-cold running caterers, bartenders, liquor store delivery boys, and waiters. The house had been scrubbed from top to bottom. The kitchen overflowed with people preparing food. Clad in navy sweats, Kitty stood in the living room, directing everyone.

Temporary bars were set up in the foyer and the den. The dining room table, stretched to its limit with inserts, had been covered with a gigantic, festive tablecloth, and sterling silver flatware. It stood proud and ready to present the scrumptious buffet. Platters, pulled from cupboards, were washed and ready to carry hot and cold hors d'oeuvres among the crowd expected to invade his space in the early afternoon.

Harry bundled up in fleece sweats and a down jacket, climbed in his SUV, and sped away. He drove around for an hour, stopping for breakfast at the mom-and-pop diner nearby. With nowhere to go, he turned the car toward Hartford and the barn. At least it would be quiet there.

After punching in his code, he opened the door, and headed for the rink. He flipped on the lights. The Zamboni had been through and the pristine ice beckoned him. He loved to be the first one on clean ice, leaving his tracks on the smooth surface.

He lugged his skates from his locker and went for a spin. Careful not to exert himself, he glided along, forward, then backward, lifting a leg, and ending in a twirl. Harry'd been on ice since he was eight. Memories of speed skating contests on a pond in the woods returned. He smiled. From the get-go, little Harry Edwards had been the fastest boy on ice in his small hometown. His parents, always stretching a buck to feed a family of five, saved enough to get him a second-hand pair of ice skates for Christmas.

It had been love at first skate. When it got dark, they'd go searching for him in the woods. There he'd be, twirling and racing along the frozen pond. Now, that would come to an end. His heart grew heavy.

Short of breath after three laps, Harry hit the bench. Recollections of fantastic shots he'd blocked marched through his mind. Then came the image of that last save, the one that had taken his career, his livelihood. He could almost feel the pain in his neck again. He touched the scar and remembered the panic, mixed with the excruciating agony, when he couldn't breathe.

They'd done a tracheotomy right in the arena before hauling him to the hospital. He awoke hooked up every which way to machines. A small, warm hand, resting in his, had brought him around. Kitty had flown up from D.C. She'd stayed by his side for the first three weeks, giving the gallery over to her assistant.

Gratitude for her loyalty again filled his heart. Though he'd never admit it, Harry'd been scared out of his mind. Kitty had soothed and calmed him. The doctors reassured him he wasn't going to die, and that he'd be able to breathe on his own just fine soon enough.

It wasn't until training started, and he ran into trouble, that the doctors admitted his life wasn't going to be exactly the same. They couldn't predict the level of restriction his salvaged windpipe would impose on his game. Hell, they thought it a miracle he was alive.

The images in his memory faded. Harry stared at the empty rink and stands. His heart squeezed. Nothing could replace the cheering of the crowd, especially when he'd blocked a goal or taken out an opponent. The noise had pumped him up like a shot of adrenaline. For a few seconds, he was Harry Edwards, king of the rink.

Emotion rose like a tidal wave in his chest. His eyes stung. Unable to tamp it down, Harry put his hands to his face and sobbed. Leaning against the railing, he cried. He'd lost his career. What would happen to his marriage?

The creaking of a door interrupted his pity party. He wiped his face on his sleeve and sat up. It was Coach Timmons.

"Saw a car. Thought it might be you."

"Yeah?" Harry replied.

"Can't imagine any of the other guys coming in here to skate on a day off."

Harry grinned. "Got that right."

Stan Timmons eased down next to Harry.

"How are you doing?"

"Been better. I'm okay. I guess."

"Gonna take that scout job?"

Harry shook his head. "Not if I want to stay married."

Coach nodded. "I see. The traveling. Right?"

"Right."

"Any other plans?"

"Nope."

Coach pursed his lips. "I might be able to do something for you."

"Really?" Harry turned his gaze to his coach.

"Yeah. Let me make some calls. Might be here in Hartford, though. Where's your wife working?"

"D.C."

"Oh, yeah. Anything I can dig up would be here."

"At least I'd be in one place."

Coach Timmons slapped Harry on the shoulder. "Okay then. I'll make some calls and get back to you. Merry Christmas, by the way."

"Merry Christmas, Coach."

Stan Timmons ambled off toward his office. Harry took off his skates, jammed them back in his locker, and washed his face. He got in the car, took a deep breath, and returned to the chaos that was his home. What would Kitty say to an opportunity that kept him in Hartford? Would he have to sell his beloved home and become permanently "Mr. Kitty" in Washington? He sighed and put the car in gear.

Chapter Four

When Harry walked in, his house was abuzz with workers. The sound of the door chimes drew his attention. He opened to find a man he had never seen before.

"And you are?"

"The piano player," the man at the door replied.

"Come in, come in." Harry stepped aside, ushering the stranger into his home. "Right this way."

"Do you have any preference for music?"

"Just Christmas stuff."

"I get that. But I mean religious or secular?"

"No madrigals, hymns, dirges or Gregorian chants. Something fun. In the spirit," Harry said.

Fun. He barely choked out that word. Would anything, outside of sex with his wife, ever be a good time again?

"Got it." The man sat down at the upright, stretched his hands and played scales.

Everyone warms up. Pianists, singers, hockey players...but he'd never warm up again. Emotion grabbed his chest. He coughed and coughed.

"Darling? Are you all right?" Kitty asked. "Sherman, get him a glass of water. Please."

Someone else Harry didn't know strode up to him with a small tumbler. Harry nodded, took the glass and sipped.

"Good." Kitty said, planting a quick kiss on Harry's lips. "Time to dress," she said, taking him by the hand.

The couple climbed the stairs to their boudoir and shut the door. Harry sank down on the bed, then fell back flat.

"Harry! Don't fall asleep! The party starts in half an hour."

"Just a little shuteye?"

Kitty sat next to him. "This is getting you down, isn't it?"

"Really? You mean losing my entire livelihood in three months isn't a good enough reason to feel like shit?"

"Of course it is. But tonight? It's Christmas Eve. Can't we look at all we have and try to be grateful? Can't we toast with our friends and family to our good fortune?"

"Good fortune? What good fortune? One fucking slapshot and I'm out to pasture. I'm thirty-three, Kitty. Thirty-three! Not forty-five. I'm not over the hill. But I am now, all because of that stupid, fucking surgery."

"That stupid fucking surgery saved your life," she pointed out.

"Life? What life? Life is over for me."

Her eyebrows rose and her eyes watered. "Harry Edwards! Don't you ever say such a thing to me again! Your life is not over. You have me. Our marriage. Our future children. And another career. We just have to figure out what that is."

"Easy for you to say. Your career is on the rise. I'm finished. Done. Dumped. Out with the trash."

She bent over to hug him. "I know you feel that way, but you'll see. Things'll get better. At least we have each other and money in the bank. That's more than most people can say."

"Fucking optimist," he muttered, rolling over on his side.

She patted his back. "Why don't I lay out your clothes while you take a short nap? Then you can change and join the party. Okay?"

He nodded. "Thanks."

Kitty disappeared into the bathroom. Harry closed his eyes. Strains of popular Christmas carols floated up to the second floor. Harry mouthed the words almost automatically. After a gazillion Christmas pageants in school, he knew all the lyrics by heart.

The First Noel, then *Silver Bells...*one by one, religious carols alternated with secular ones. Harry's eyes drifted shut, but the songs continued to play in his head. He loved Christmas carols. When they were first married, he and Kitty tagged along with a group of neighborhood carolers. Since he'd made the big-time, they'd sold their tiny starter house and bought this elegant abode. The switch in neighborhoods brought an end to the holiday tradition. He'd missed it.

The click of the bathroom door startled him. Kitty emerged, dressed in the most beautiful forest green velvet, floor-length dress. The scoop neck highlighted her graceful shoulders and ample bosom. God, she took his breath away.

"Great, you look great," he murmured.

"Thanks." She bent to kiss him and was out the door before he could comment further. His eyelids grew heavy.

A hand jostled his shoulder. "Get up. Harry. Time to get up." He cracked sleepy lids to spy his wife at his side.

"Darling, the party is going great. Please get dressed and come downstairs. Everyone is asking for you."

Harry managed a weak smile, pushed up on his elbows and threw off the covers. Kitty hugged him. “The party’s not the same without you. Hurry, darling.”

He nodded. She called him “darling” when she worried about him. Hey, he was fine, physically. One sharp-eyed glance at Kitty gave it away. Her eyebrows knitted, and she’d pulled her lower lip between her teeth. He smoothed her hair with his palm.

“I’ll be right down.”

“Good. Love you,” she said and was gone in a shot.

Sounds of singing met his ears. The piano sounded good—the voices, not so much. He chuckled. Wasn’t a decent, tune-carrier on the entire team. A quick splash of water on his face and then he ran a comb through his short hair. Harry buttoned his flannel shirt, zipped up his cords, and headed for the stairs. When he appeared at the top, a shout went up.

“Harry!”

His rowdy teammates held up glasses and cheered. It wasn’t about what had happened, because they didn’t know. His conversation with Coach Timmons had been private. The goofballs playing on the Huskies did that for him every year.

Harry’s parents now resided in Florida, so they weren’t at the party but Kitty’s were. They greeted Harry with hugs and sympathetic looks. *Shit! They know!* He couldn’t expect Kitty to keep the bad news from her family.

He exchanged high fives, butt pats, and shoulder slaps with his teammates as he made his way to the bar. At least he could have a few good belts now and watch his teammates stay dry. He exchanged greetings with the neighbors, then sidled up to a group of five Huskies who were discussing the next game.

"The Falcons have won their last five games," Buzzy said.

"Philly's always been hard to beat," said their star forward.

"That fuckin' forward, Darren something?" asked their number two defenseman.

"He's been their lead scorer all season."

The men turned slightly to face Harry. "Harry, got any ideas how to rock them?"

"Well. Darren's not God. Every man's got a weakness. I remember last year..."

Harry launched into a description of the close game they played last January, then chucked in advice. The men hung on his words. Glancing up, he noticed Kitty leaning against the archway, drink in hand, smiling, watching.

"What about Pierre?"

"Pierre? That pussy?" Harry laughed and returned his gaze to his men.

After his third scotch, he found a comfortable chair. It was ten and most of the guests had left. His buddies had to be in bed early. Some had kids who'd be up at the crack of dawn. Before they returned to their own homes, they'd hugged and swore they'd beat the crap out of Philly.

Kitty approached, balancing a plate piled high with food.

"Here."

"Thank you. So much jaw flappin', I forgot to eat."

Kitty settled her little rump on the arm of the chair. Harry dug in, picking up a skewer with ham and pineapple.

"Did you have a good time?"

His mouth full, he nodded.

"I thought so. Told you."

He swallowed. "You did. But this is the last one."

"What?"

"Who knows where I'll be or what I'll be doing next year. But I sure as hell won't be a member of the Huskies."

HARRY FELL ASLEEP BEFORE Kitty came to bed. After a restless night, he awoke at four, managing to slide out from under the covers without disturbing his wife. Feeling his way through his dark bedroom, he headed for the living room. With the heat turned down, the house had cooled. He made a fire in the fireplace and plugged in the Christmas tree. Nabbing the soft afghan that decorated the arm of the sofa, he wrapped it around himself.

Sitting back, Harry watched the small flames grow. He turned to study the tree. About seven feet tall, and perfectly decorated by Kitty, its lights winked at him. Never much for sentiment, still, Harry's gaze stopped at the most meaningful ornaments. There was the frog on skis he gave to her after their first ski weekend. The two hearts intertwined he presented to her after the first time they made love. The tree symbolized their life together. His eyes wetted.

Many questions swirled through his mind. He struggled, in vain, for answers. He loved his wife, his home, and hockey. Was there any way he could continue to have all three?

Kitty deserved to keep her gallery in D. C. But truth be told, her absence hadn't been getting easier. Puck Bunnies tempted him on the road. He resisted but wondered how long he'd be able to hold out. On a long, hard road trip, loneliness crushed him. He'd spend an hour or more on the phone with Kitty. They'd even had Skype sex, but nothing beat the feel of her skin or the warm reassurance of her snuggle.

The scouting job? Nope, it wasn't for him—too far away from hockey action, and too much traveling. Hotel rooms depressed him. They showed no sign of life, of personality, nothing but sterile, empty spaces.

He stretched out on the sofa and shut his eyes. Images of a pregnant Kitty and babies flitted through his imagination, followed by screaming triplets, smelly diapers, and Harry at the end of his rope. He sat up with a start, sweat beading his forehead.

He could face the fiercest forwards, the biggest, brutish hockey players knocking him into the boards or on his ass, but taking care of a child terrified him. He knew hockey, not kids. What did he know about being a parent? Zip, zilch, nada, nothing—he was totally ignorant.

He'd wanted them five years ago when he was too dumb to know better, but now? Life would be chaotic. Private time with Kitty would go out the window, along with their sex life. He shuddered. Having kids couldn't save him. He'd have to save himself.

The heat from the fire raised the room temperature to almost comfortable. He tucked the blanket under his thighs and fell asleep.

"Ho, ho, ho, Santa. Time to get up," a fake deep voice said in his ear.

Harry yawned and rubbed his eyes. Wrapped in a blue plaid flannel robe, Kitty stood before him, beaming.

"Merry Christmas," she said, holding a small, rectangular gift in one hand and a cup of steaming hot coffee in the other.

"Merry Christmas yourself, Missus. Thanks for the java." He took the mug and eyed the other item.

"This is for you." She shoved it into his empty hand. Harry put down his drink and unwrapped it. Inside was a gold watch.

"I kind of figured you deserved it for your years in hockey," she said, joining him on the sofa.

He fastened it around his thick wrist. "Fits perfect. It's great. Thank you," he said, eying the timepiece from all angles before pulling his wife to him for a kiss. Tossing the covering aside, he pushed to his feet and headed for the tree. After rummaging through the packages there, he plucked out the small ones he got at the jewelry store.

"Here you go. Merry Christmas, Kitty. And thanks for being the best wife ever." He handed her the presents.

She tore open the paper. Her face lit up like a thousand stars when she saw the diamonds.

"They're real. Honest. They're real." He nodded.

"Oh, my God! Harry! They're too much. This is too expensive," she said, waving the diamond tennis bracelet in his face. "You've got to take it back. We can't afford it now."

"Do you like it?"

"Of course. Who wouldn't? But..."

He put his finger to her lips. "It's not too expensive. We can afford it. As long as you like it."

"But your salary?"

"They're buying out my contract. Even without that. Believe me, we're not hurting."

"It's beautiful. Can you fasten it for me?" she asked, turning grateful eyes to him.

He chuckled. "Of course. There. Perfect fit. It looks amazing on you."

She gave him a passionate kiss. Harry eased her down on the sofa and made love to her.

When they'd reached completion, Harry made another pot of coffee and the couple opened more gifts. Harry donned one of the flannel shirts, smiling at his reflection in the mirror. Kitty wore the diamond earrings. She scrambled up eggs and reheated leftover ham. Harry consulted the television and set up a movie lineup for the day.

They didn't make any calls or even get dressed. They cuddled up in front of the tube, ate their fill, drank champagne, and made love.

In the middle of *It's a Wonderful Life*, the phone rang. Harry made a face but loped across the room and picked up his cell. It was Coach Timmons.

"Sorry to interrupt your Christmas, Harry, but I've got someone I want you to meet. Do you have time tomorrow?"

"Sure, Coach. Who is it?"

"I'll pick you up at ten. Let me fill you in on the way."

"Okay. Works for me. Merry Christmas."

"Thanks, Harry. Same to you."

Harry cocked his head to the side. Not a secretive person, Coach Timmons was all hush-hush on the phone. His behavior piqued Harry's curiosity.

"Who was that?"

"Coach. Wants to see me tomorrow."

"Oh. Hope it's good news."

"Me, too." If she only knew. Maybe he wasn't finished after all?

THE NEXT MORNING, HARRY donned his new Black Watch plaid shirt and paced by the window. It was quarter to ten, his nerves had hit high alert about ten minutes earlier. He'd managed to snarf down some leftover ham and a couple of rolls with butter.

Now he nursed a second cup of coffee as he stood, watching for the coach's car. A few flakes from the trees swirled around, then down.

"It's windy. Bundle up," Kitty said, as she walked by, carrying serving pieces.

The clean-up after the party took two days. In the past, he'd been playing in Hartford or on the road, so he couldn't help. But not today.

"When you get back, I've got a list for you."

"Okay," he said.

The sudden beep from a car snagged his attention. "Coach is here," he called out to his wife.

"Good luck." She blew him a kiss.

Harry was out the door and down the stairs in a flash. He and the coach exchanged greetings.

"Where are we headed?"

"You'll see. The man you're going to meet is named Buster Callahan. He runs a program at the Veteran's Memorial Rink, here in West Hartford."

"Program?"

"Yeah. I'll let him tell you."

Timmons pulled into the parking lot and stopped the car. As they walked through the icy wind to the entrance, Coach rested his hand on Harry's shoulder.

"All I ask is that you keep an open mind."

Coach's words worried Harry. What was so terrible that he should keep an open mind? When people said that, it never ended up good.

Buster Callahan greeted them. After hand-shaking all around, they proceeded to the rink.

"We've been running a summer hockey camp here for teens," Buster began.

Harry raised his eyebrows.

"We had a volunteer coach, one of the dads, but the kids complained. Besides, he's moving next week. We want to expand the program, run it as an after school and a summer camp. We need someone experienced to handle it. Someone the kids'll respect. You fit the bill perfectly, Mr. Edwards."

"Harry, please."

"Okay. You're it. You're top of the line. I'm sure with you coaching, we'd have more kids signing up than we could handle."

"'You want me to coach kids?"

"Not little kids. Teens. Some are quite talented. They might even end up on the Huskies."

Silence. *Kids. Teens. Bratty, snotty, insolent teens. Not on your life.*

"Mr. Callahan..."

"Buster, Please."

"I don't think I'm suited to work with kids. I'm kinda rough around the edges. My language alone would have most mothers passed out on the floor."

Buster laughed. “That’s okay. The kids expect that. And the mothers won’t be here when you’re teaching. These are good kids. Respectful.”

“What about the ones who aren’t.”

“We’d be giving you complete control. Anyone who talks back or doesn’t behave properly...you’d have the authority to kick them out of the program.”

Harry smiled. “Good. ’Cause that’s the only way they’ll learn. You have to be tough.”

“Exactly! That’s what we’re looking for. A serious coach. Someone who’s demanding and doesn’t let the kids get away with a lot of shit.”

“That’s Harry,” Coach Timmons put in.

“Salary? I hope this isn’t a volunteer job.”

Buster laughed. “You’ve got to be kidding? A man of your experience and accomplishment? We’d never expect you to work for nothing. Salary would be a percentage of the enrollment. The after school is going to be pricey. About two grand per semester. Say we get thirty kids, that’s sixty grand. We’d give you forty percent. Or twenty-four grand. After school is from three to five, five days a week. So you’d be making that for ten hours of work a week, times two semesters.”

“And the prep work before and after, too.”

“Of course. I know that’s a drop-in-the-bucket for a star like you. We’d pay more for the summer programs. Think of the lives you’d be changing.”

“How many weeks?”

“January through May. July and August, then September through November. All in all, you’d make about a hundred grand a year, including the summer program.”

Buster handed Harry a card. "Here's a free pass for you and a friend. It's good until June. Stop by, try out the rink. I can arrange for you to meet some of the kids who are in the program now, if you'd like."

"Thanks," Harry said, shoving the card in his back pocket. "Let me think about it."

"We're aiming to have the top program in the country, Harry. And with you here coaching? We're a slam dunk."

"Thanks for the vote of confidence."

"Whadda ya think?" Coach Timmons asked.

"Have to think about it. Talk it over with my wife."

"Sure, sure. We'd like to be able to announce you as our new coach by the end of the week. I'm betting, as soon as it gets out you're coaching, we get flooded with kids wanting to sign up."

"And what if you don't?"

"Are you saying the kids around here wouldn't give their right arm to learn to play hockey from you? You're kidding, right?" Buster's eyebrows shot up.

Harry laughed. "I'm no god."

"You are to hockey fans."

Harry turned and stuck out his hand. Buster took it. "Thank you, Buster, for the offer. I'll get back to you in a couple of days."

"That's all I can ask."

The coach and Buster shook hands.

"My son's in that program," Coach Timmons said.

"Really?"

"Yep."

"So, this wasn't out of the blue. You didn't call him up and beg him to hire me, did you?"

"Didn't have to. Minute I mentioned you might be looking for something, he jumped on it."

Coach broke the silence that had settled in as they headed back to Harry's house.

"Think you'll take the job?"

"Beats scouting."

"Won't pay nearly as much."

"Doesn't matter. Pays not the thing."

"Travel a problem?"

Harry nodded. "That and being away from the game. I've been on the ice since I was eight."

"That's a long time."

"Yeah. At least with the coaching job, I'd be skating every day."

"You'd be a good teacher."

"If I take the job, I ain't goin' easy on your kid."

The coach laughed. "Good. Robbie needs a strong hand. Does that mean you'll take it?"

"Not sayin' yes, an' not sayin' no. Gotta talk to Kitty."

"Sure. No problem."

"Thanks for recommending me."

The coach nodded.

Harry invited Stan for lunch, but he begged off, citing family time before they got back to hockey. Harry trudged up the steps. *Out to pasture. Is this what a retired racehorse feels like? Of course, he goes to stud. That's a different matter. No one's offering to pay me to knock up women.* Harry chuckled to himself, wondering what that would be like.

"What's so funny?" Kitty asked, greeting him at the door.

Harry sensed color invading his cheeks. "Nothing."

"Not nothing. You're blushing. You never blush."

"What's for lunch?"

"Clam chowder and lobster salad."

Harry's appetite kicked into gear. "Sounds great."

"So? What happened?"

"Let's eat first."

Chapter Five

KITTY CLEARED AWAY the lunch dishes. Harry bellied up to the sink to load the dishwasher.

"Coach told me to go with them on the trip to Philly."

"When do you leave?"

"Tomorrow."

"Make sure you get what's coming to you," Kitty said, putting placemats in a drawer.

"It's all in the contract, hon. Nothing to worry about. I spoke to Mark. He said Timmons placed me on the long-term injured reserve list."

"What does that mean?"

"Means they gotta pay my salary for the duration of my contract."

"And that is?"

"I've got four years left. Three mil a year."

"Not bad," she said.

"I suppose. Feels wrong taking the money and not playing," Harry said, closing the machine and turning it on.

"It's your right. It's not like they don't have the money."

"True, true." He sighed. "Where's the paper?"

"On the sofa."

Harry retired to the living room. Kitty joined him. Looking down he noticed she wore the diamond tennis bracelet.

"Who says you can't wear diamonds at home?" she asked, fingering the jewels.

He kissed her.

"So, are you going to take the coaching job?" she asked, tucking her legs beneath her.

He pursed his lip. "Probably not."

"The scouting job?"

He shook his head.

"Then what?"

"I don't have a fucking clue." He rose and headed for the stairs.

Kitty went to the window and watched the birds. Harry had put out a feeder and the hungry little creatures were filling their bellies. She gnawed on her lip, worry seeping into her heart. When Harry gave her the green light to take over the gallery, they had had to work things out between them. There had been tense days of arguing, stony silence, and slamming out of the house. After the drama subsided, they had discussed their differences and worked out a plan.

Dazzled by Harry upon first meeting, she'd grown to love the real man, the one behind the hockey fame and glamour. He'd been everything she'd wanted in a husband. When he proposed, she'd been over the moon, mad in love, and convinced they'd be together forever.

Then one injury had razed their finely-constructed scheme. Kitty admitted to herself that so much time apart had worn thin. Although she had no alternative, she'd hoped to talk to Harry about changing things. She missed him so much it hurt.

Now everything had been ripped apart, as if by a tornado. To Kitty, it represented an opportunity. She'd seized on the idea of his not playing hockey and their spending more time together with great hope. The scouting offer scared the crap out of her—more travel? Their marriage would be doomed.

He'd turned away from the idea of having children and being a stay-at-home dad. Then he scuttled the chance to coach and stay in West Hartford. His negative attitude and closed mind dashed dreams of rearranging their life to be more normal.

She headed for the kitchen to put up a pot of coffee. He'd leave tomorrow with the team, but for how long? They had to settle things tonight. Maybe Harry had been right that divorce was the only answer. If he refused to consider viable alternatives, what choice did she have? Living with an angry man who'd shut himself up in his house or tag along after her, resenting every step, would bring a happy marriage to a bitter end.

Was it better to have a friendly divorce now or watch their relationship crumble to acrimonious ashes? Tears stung at the back of her eyes. There must be something she could do. She added milk and sugar to her mug and ambled back to the living room.

The gallery had grown. Shows were bringing in a decent crowd, and she'd covered all her expenses from income earned this year—a first. Harry had provided funds to make up the difference in the past. She couldn't completely walk away from it at this point. Kitty had worked hard to get it up and running, now was no time to quit.

She sipped her coffee as the bare-bones of a plan formed in her head. Concessions, big ones from both sides, would be needed for her idea to work. Her brows knitted. Harry had not been in a compromising mood lately. She had to give him time to adjust to the change in his life. But time was the one thing they didn't have. He'd be off on the road and she'd return to Washington. Decisions had to be made now. She picked up the phone and headed to the den for privacy.

HARRY LAY IN BED, TRYING to read. Finally, he put the book down. He pushed to his feet and stared out the window. Snow blanketed the trees, freezing into a crystalline coating on even the tiniest branches. The sky hung heavy with gray clouds. As he gazed at the landscape, he frowned.

What the hell was he going to do with his life now? Tag along after the team, watching them from the sidelines for a couple of months, while his marriage deteriorated? Or would he take the scouting job and get a divorce before his being gone turned them sour toward each other?

And that stupid coaching job! How ridiculous to turn him into a babysitter for a bunch of pimply faced, horny teens. He knew the hockey forward and backward, but they'd be more interested in the latest video game, getting laid, and smoking pot than paying attention to him.

Harry "Deke" Edwards, washed up, a man without a life. He watched the birds, industriously combing the frozen trees and ground for food—hell, at least they had jobs. He shook his head. This damn pity party had to stop. Wound-licking didn't make him feel better or solve his problems. Only jerks sat around sucking their thumbs and feeling sorry for themselves.

Time to do something. Make a decision. His lips compressed into a thin line. First step would be following along with the team on this road trip. He yanked his small suitcase down from the closet and rummaged through his dresser. Time to pack. He'd think of something to say to Kitty to put her off until he'd had time to ponder life. He stopped.

What about Kitty? And the gallery? He had no answer. If he lost her, then he'd truly have nothing, but he'd be damned if he'd live the rest of his life as "Mr. Kitty" in D.C. He folded his clothes and laid them in the valise, then grabbed his spare Dopp kit and shoved it in. He'd have to leave at seven tomorrow morning to make the plane to Philly.

The aroma of something good lured him to the top of the stairs.

"What's cookin'?" he yelled down toward the kitchen.

"Heating up some leftover roast beef and that apple pie. Hungry?"

"I am now," he said descending to the first floor.

While Kitty bustled about, gathering the food, Harry set out the silverware. He opened a bottle of Malbec. They took their places at the kitchen table.

"You're leaving early tomorrow, right?" Kitty asked.

He nodded, cutting off a piece of the succulent meat.

"We have to discuss some stuff." She hesitated, her lip trembling a touch as she put down her fork. "Where do we go from here?"

"I don't know." He cupped her cheek and met her gaze with his. "We'll work it out."

"I need more than that, Harry. This is a crisis. Talk to me."

He put down his fork. "I don't have any answers. I thought that, after this road trip, on New Year's, we could talk about where we go from here. Maybe by then, we'll have direction."

"You want me to wait?"

"It's only a week."

"True." She cast her gaze to her plate.

Harry took her hand. "We can work it out, Kitty." His lips spoke, but his mind didn't agree.

"Can we?" She raised her eyes to his.

"Of course we can." Emotion gathered in his chest.

"We'll see." She turned her attention back to her food.

That wasn't the answer Harry expected. Had Kitty lost hope? He'd been acting like an idiot, moping around, worrying only about himself. How could he blame her?

"What's happening at the gallery?" he asked, stuffing a forkful of mashed potatoes into his mouth.

"Nothing too much. We're finally in the black this year."

"That's great."

"Thanks. I have plans to expand, sort of. Do more shows, find new artists."

Beautiful and brainy, too. How did he get so lucky? Harry took her hand. "I'm proud of you."

"Thanks." She put down her fork. "Look, if you want to take that scouting job, I understand. The team is everything. Always has been. We could get a friendly divorce. If that's what you want. I don't want to stand in your way." The color drained from her face.

Coming from her mouth, the word *divorce* terrified him. For a moment, words froze in his throat. She'd read his mind. The team had been his life until he met her. He'd thought it had settled into a fifty-fifty deal, with the team and Kitty splitting his heart.

In an instant, hearing her words clarified everything. He took her hand.

"The team isn't everything to me. You are," he whispered, his voice hoarse with emotion.

Tears spilled over onto her cheeks as she raised his hand to her lips.

"Do you want a divorce?" he asked.

She shook her head.

"Then let's keep the original plan. I'll think about it on the road. You at home. At New Years, we'll talk."

"Okay," she muttered, nodding.

His palms sweated, but the fluttering in his heart stopped. As easily as he'd thought about divorce before, once she said it, he realized a divorce would be a huge bomb in his life, blowing up what he loved most. If he needed to move to D.C. to keep Kitty, he'd figure it out.

"I can't lose you. Please. I just can't." He pulled her onto his lap and hugged her tight.

She buried her face in his comfy shoulder and sobbed.

AFTER A QUIET FAREWELL, Harry drove to Hartford. He boarded the aircraft with the rest of the team. Would this be his last time? He sat next to Buzzy and peered out the tiny window. The snow had stopped, but it had turned colder.

The plane climbed steadily, offering a view of snowy houses before it reached cruising altitude. Once it leveled off, there wasn't much to see. Buzzy buried his nose in Sports Illustrated.

"It isn't even the swimsuit issue," Harry muttered.

"Nope. But there's a piece here on Ron Duguay."

"Duguay? He still alive?"

"Yep. He coached in the minors for four years. You think about that?"

"Nah." The minors, what would he want with the minor leagues? A bunch of guys who could either shoot straight or defend but not both.

"Turnin' your nose up at the minors? Didn't you start there?"

"Only for one season. Huskies drafted me after I kicked fuckin' butt in Scranton."

"Duguay jumped right from amateur hockey to the Rangers."

Harry read over his buddy's shoulder.

"He set a Ranger record for the fastest goal at the start of a game," Buzzy went on.

"Yeah?"

"Nine seconds," the winger said, whistling through his teeth.

"That's impressive. Did I ever tell you, MacConnell, about the time I... Harry began.

Buzzy closed the magazine and turned his attention to his teammate. One player sitting in front of them pushed up, turning his head to listen in.

When the plane landed at Philadelphia International Airport, the team boarded a private bus to the hotel. The men checked in before they headed to the arena to practice. The team chowed down at the barn before the game.

Since he wasn't scheduled to play, Harry'd watch the game from the Huskies' private box. Before game time, Harry, dressed in a suit, hung around the locker room.

"Watch out for that dickwad, Darren," Harry whispered to Bastien "Bass" Javier, the defenseman taking Harry's spot.

"Darren?" The younger man's brows knitted as he shot a quizzical glance Harry's way.

"Yeah. That asshole is their biggest scorer. They pass to him before every goal."

Bass nodded before he hit the chute with the rest of the team. Off the roster, like a bad boy, Harry headed for the box. What the fuck! Why was he even there if he wasn't going to play?

As he watched the game, he noticed Coach Timmons gnawing on a fingernail. With a new man at defense, the whole balance of the team was off. With Harry in that slot, the Huskies hummed like a fine-tuned violin. But now? Hell, there'd be a whole lotta adjusting and fucked up plays until Bastien hit a rhythm with the others.

Harry cheered the good plays and booed the bad calls. At intermission, he joined the players in the locker room. Bass Javier plopped down on a bench and sucked down water. Harry sidled up to him.

"That fucker Darren. You gotta watch him. Keep your eye on him. Someone else brings it down, that asshole crosses over, and right when he's in front, wham! He gets a pass and puts it in. Get your ass on him."

Bass nodded as Harry went on. When Stan Timmons addressed the team, Harry moved to a corner to listen. Was this his last pep talk? A lump formed in Harry's throat. When the team filed down the chute to the ice, Harry hung back. He blinked rapidly, wiped his nose with his handkerchief, and took a deep breath before taking his place in the box.

As play resumed, Buzzy took a perfect shot that was deflected by a Falcon defenseman. The same man bounced him into the boards. Harry jumped up out of his seat, yelling for a foul call. When he didn't get it, anger steamed up his chest, he itched to get revenge on the ice. And he'd have done it, too, if he'd been playing. Watching from the box sucked big time. Harry jerked open a bottle of water and washed his rage down.

The Huskies lost the game with Philly, and the next one in New York, too. By the third game, in Baltimore, frustration had turned to desperation. Competitive spirit morphed into sheer hatred of the Baltimore Bulldogs. Harry nicknamed them the *Baltimore Bullies* for their dirty playing. Harry shouted encouragement from the bench.

Bass blocked the Bulldogs hotshot forward, knocking him into the boards and stole the puck. He raced down the ice, then shot a perfect pass to Buzz, who put it away. The goal bucked up the Huskies, who turned the tide, beating Baltimore three to two.

AFTER THE GAME, COACH Timmons called Harry into the injury room, a substitute office.

"Sit down," he said. "We're wrapping up the details with your agent about the contract buyout. You have a choice. You can ride out the rest of the season with us, or you can move on."

Harry nodded, casting his gaze to the floor.

"Mind if I give you a little advice?"

"Please."

"You're thirty-three, right?" Again, Harry nodded. "You've made it past some players, age-wise. Retirement comes to all of us, eventually. It's fifteen years for me, but I remember like it was yesterday. It's not easy to take, but hell, it's a medical and you're in good shape. Count yourself lucky. Cheer up. You're young for anything else. There's a shitload of stuff you can do."

"None of it's what I want."

"Hell, man. Stop complaining! You've got two good offers I know of. Probably could have more, if you'd look into it."

"Maybe."

"If you keep up this bad attitude, you'll lose your friends, your wife, everything. Harry, pull yourself together. Play the cards you've been dealt. Make lemonade out of lemons. How many more stupid, dumbass fucking clichés do I have to throw at you?" Stan Timmons cracked a smile.

"You're right. It's just that I wasn't expecting it. I thought I could play into my forties, like some other guys."

"That's the exception, not the rule."

"I guess."

"Got money?"

Harry nodded.

"Well, hell, man. What more do you want? In the prime of life and enough money to not have to work, right? You've got choices. You can do shit just because you want to. It's a gift. A gift not many receive."

"Never thought of it that way."

"That's the way it is. Be positive. Find a new path."

"Thanks, Coach."

"Let me know if you want to travel out the season with us."

"I will." Harry rose. The men embraced, and the coach slapped Harry on the shoulder as he left. Coach's words tumbled again and again through Harry's brain as he changed and headed for the bus. Was he right? Did Harry have a great life ahead or was he finished?

A tired team climbed on the plane for the flight home from Baltimore at the end of their road trip. It was December thirtieth. The men talked about getting home to their families and quiet New Year's celebrations. Harry didn't hear, his mind was elsewhere. He slipped into the seat Buzzy saved for him.

As the bus made its way to Hartford, Harry made one decision. The pain of traveling with the team and watching from the box overwhelmed him. No way could he continue to pretend he was a Husky. Riding shotgun wasn't in Harry's wheelhouse. A man of action, he'd always been the one making hockey happen, not cheering from the sidelines. He hated the idea of being a fifth wheel, watching his team play, helpless, unable to contribute to a victory.

As the bus rolled along the highway, Harry considered the options set before him. He'd have to pick one or come up with something else himself. Clueless, he bounced back and forth between the scouting offer and coaching the kids. Or he could become a house husband and raise a brood of little hockey players.

"Got plans?" Buzzy asked him.

"Nothing much. You?"

"Oh, yeah. I'm gonna pop the big one to Brenda."

"Don't tell me what you're doing with your dick, Buzzy. Some things should remain private."

"I wasn't talking about sex, you dickwad! The big one, question. Propose, you idiot!"

Harry laughed. "Oh, I see. Sorry."

"Sometimes you can be so dense. Get your head out of your ass. You know what you oughta do? Oughta have a dozen kids, so you could think about somebody else for a change," Buzzy said, crossing his arms over his chest.

"I said I was sorry."

"You're too damn touchy these days."

"You would be, too, if you were forced outta hockey by some stupid asshole's slapshot."

Harry turned away, facing the window.

"Is that it? I wondered why you weren't playing."

"Yeah. I'm being put out to pasture. No wind. Can't skate. Can't run. They made my windpipe smaller and I can't get enough air," Harry said, his voice low.

"Oh shit, man. Fuck! That sucks. You're really off the team?"

"Can't play. What's the point of traveling around with the Huskies?"

Buzzy grabbed Harry and hugged him. "Fuck it, Deke. I had no idea."

"Yeah, well, that's the way I wanted it. Guess I can't hide it forever."

"The guys should know."

"They've probably figured it out by now. Seeing as I passed out on the ice in my last game."

"There was some talk."

"About me?"

"Just guessing."

"You can set 'em straight."

"If you want me to."

Harry nodded. "Go ahead. Doesn't matter now anyway."

"Gonna miss you," Buzzy said, his voice husky.

"Don't go there," Harry said, holding up his hand.

The bus from the airport arrived at the arena. The men pushed forward while Harry hung back. He was the last one off. Kitty waved from the car. He smiled as he made his way to her.

Leaning over, he kissed her.

"Good trip?" she asked, putting the vehicle in gear.

"Not really. We split. Lost in Philly and New York. Won in Baltimore."

"At least you didn't lose them all."

"True."

Conversation veered toward dinner and their plans for New Year's Eve.

"I don't want to celebrate this year," he said.

"What?"

"I mean, let's skip the Sullivans' party. Okay?"

"Okay."

"Just get a couple of movies, some bubbly and order in Chinese. Just you and me."

"If that's what you want," she said, keeping her eyes on the road.

"Did you want to go to the party?"

"It's okay. I like their parties, but it won't kill me to miss it."

"You understand?" he asked.

"Of course. But we do need to return to the land of the living eventually," she put in.

He chuckled.

Kitty turned into their semi-circular driveway. The smell of good food met Harry at the door. He took his bag upstairs, washed up, and met her at the table.

"Roast turkey. My favorite," he said, picking up the carving knife.

"And turkey sandwiches for tomorrow."

They focused on their food, avoiding conversation. When they finished, Harry cleared the table.

"They're planning to throw a little party for you at Veteran's Memorial Rink tomorrow. Around lunchtime."

"Lunchtime? We have turkey sandwiches," Harry said.

"Those are for tomorrow night with the movies, chips, brownies, and champagne."

"Do I have to go?"

"Of course you do, you're the guest of honor."

"What if I break down?"

"Everyone'll break down with you. Come on, Harry. Don't be difficult. Coach Timmons called and said you have to be there," Kitty said, clenching her jaw.

"Okay, okay. I know I'm being an asshole. I'll go."

"Good," Kitty replied.

"You coming, too?"

"Wouldn't miss it," she said, a twinkle in her eye. Harry did the dishes while Kitty put away the food. He finished first and came up behind her, wrapping his arms around her middle. He kissed her neck.

"I think maybe the idea of having kids is a good way to go," he said, sliding his hands up over her breasts.

"Oh? Did you want to start now?" she asked.

"Why not?" he replied.

Chapter Six

At sunup, Kitty snuggled down under the comforter and pressed up against Harry. He grunted.

"Wow. You were an animal last night. Four times?" she asked.

"Yep. Can't score a goal takin' only one shot," he responded, snaking his arm around her middle and closing his eyes.

Taking a deep breath, she inhaled his warm, sleepy scent. Well satisfied, she let her mind wander. How long after ditching the diaphragm would it take to get pregnant? Surprised that Harry had taken to the idea, Kitty sighed. Unsure whether her husband would trade hockey for their marriage, she'd been living with a ball of nerves in the middle of her gut.

Unable to get back to sleep, she padded down to the kitchen. French toast occupied her thoughts, with a little ham on the side, maybe? As she cooked, baby names flitted through her mind. She hummed a favorite tune as she melted butter in the pan. The aroma of fresh coffee tempted her. She poured a mug, then added sugar and milk.

When the meal was ready, she arranged it on a tray and headed for the stairs. This would be a good time to tell Harry of her plan. Her body hummed as she climbed, slowly, balancing the plates and mug.

"Get up, Harry. Sleepyhead. Time to rise and shine."

He groaned. "I did too much rising last night. Can't a guy sleep in on a day off?"

She laughed. "French toast?"

Harry cracked an eye. "Thought something smelled good, besides you." He pushed up to a sitting position and grabbed a pillow for his lap. Kitty set the tray down gently.

"Not to sound ungrateful, but is there a reason for this grand gesture?"

"Just because I love my husband." She perched on the end of the bed.

Harry cocked an eyebrow. "Why am I thinkin' there's more to this than that?"

"The gratitude of a satisfied woman?" she replied, raising her eyebrows.

"Wipe that innocent look off your face. I've known you too long. What's up?" he asked, taking a sip of the steaming brew, then picking up his fork.

"Well, I have something to discuss with you. It's something I've been thinking about for a long time."

His eyebrows shot up. "Something bad?"

She put her hand on his arm. "No, no. Something good, real good."

"Whew. Don't do that. You scared me." He cut a piece of the luscious toast.

Kitty stared at him. Naked under the covers, with his chest exposed, he tempted her. She leaned toward him and rested her palm on his pecs.

"More? Let me finish eating first." He eyed the opening of her robe, revealing her breast.

"Maybe in a bit. First, let me tell you what happened," she said, following his gaze and closing her robe.

"Damn. You cut off the view."

"Please eat and listen."

"Shoot." He speared a piece of ham.

"I got an offer for the gallery."

"What?"

"Jefferson University approached me two months ago. First, they wanted to buy me out, but I refused."

"Buy you out? But why would you do that?"

"I wouldn't—at least not back then. Last week, they offered to partner with me. I've been thinking. Since you're giving up hockey, I'd like to be here with you. So maybe I could partner with Jefferson in D. C. then, with the money I'd get from Jefferson, I'd start a branch here in West Hartford."

"How would the partnership work? How much time would you spend in D.C.?"

"I don't know. We haven't worked that out yet. But if we have kids—"

"When we have kids," he put in.

"When we have kids, if I worked here, it would be easier. If you took the coaching job, we could tag team. You'd be home with the children in the morning. Then I could come home early and take them in the afternoon, while you're coaching."

She held her breath. Harry'd never been easy with change. And now his whole life had been turned upside down. Could he cope? He put down his fork.

"You've been thinking a lot about this."

"I talked to the doctor."

"When?"

"A couple of months ago. Right around the time Jefferson approached me."

"Weren't you going to tell me?"

"It never seemed like the right time."

He nodded. "I see."

"Are you mad?"

"Just surprised. You never keep things from me."

"Not usually. We were both keeping it from each other."

Harry chuckled. "That's it."

"What do you think?" she asked.

"I think you want me to take that coaching job."

"I do."

"I'm so proud of you. Imagine, the university wanting to muscle in on your operation."

"They're not muscling in. They figure it would be a great place to show the work of their art students, and maybe even attract more and build up the department."

"That's what they said?"

"Yes. I had no idea my little place would draw their attention."

Harry took her hand and brought it to his lips. "You're a star, Kitty. I've always said so."

She sensed color heating her cheeks.

"I think the plan is brilliant," he said.

"You do?" Her heart took flight. "Really?"

"I do," he said, finishing off his meal.

Kitty moved the tray and hugged him. "Thank you. Thank you so much."

HARRY GRINNED IN THE shower. He couldn't believe he had the stuff to make love to his wife again after breakfast. Maybe he couldn't play hockey anymore, but he could still score with Kitty.

As he dressed for the reception at Veteran's Memorial Arena, Buzzy's words came back to him. "Think about somebody else for a change, instead of yourself." His buddy shared wise words. Harry had become self-obsessed. Living with the sexiest, smartest, most beautiful woman in the world, he'd ignored her. What did his giving up hockey mean for Kitty? Of course, she'd have a plan. Kitty had been a planner from the day she was born. He chuckled.

Harry opted to ride this out, sit back and let others chart the course. He'd learn how to let go and give the wheel to someone else—his wife, and maybe that guy, Buster Callahan. He thrust his legs into his good corduroy pants, pulled a long-sleeved T-shirt over his head and plucked his sports jacket off the hanger.

"Ready, Kitty?"

"Almost," she called from her vanity.

While she applied makeup, Harry stuffed his wallet and keys into his pocket. She stood up, clad in an emerald green velour running suit. Her clear, porcelain skin shone, and her eyes sparkled.

"I swear you are the most beautiful woman in the world," he said.

She kissed him. "Thank you. Ready?"

He nodded and headed for the stairs. Emotion formed a lump in his throat, choking him. He tossed the car keys to his wife. The plows had cleaned the streets and a bit of sun melted what was left on the pavement. Kitty steered them safely on the twenty-minute trip.

She took his hand as they walked to the front door. Once inside, a huge cheer went up from his teammates. They were on the ice, skating around the perimeter. There was a big cake in the center, on a table. The men sang, "For He's a Jolly Good Fellow."

The cake was cut and pieces passed around. The players, coaches, and trainers sat together on the sidelines, talking and eating. Kitty sat with Coach Timmons and Buster Callahan. Harry glanced up at her from time to time. Though he tried with everything in him to control his emotions, his eyes watered anyway. He found the handkerchief his wife had tucked into his jacket pocket.

Buzzy and a few of his teammates teared up, too. Harry passed the hanky around.

"Gonna have kids, maybe?" Buzzy asked.

"And that's your business?"

"Just wondering."

"Wonder all you like," Harry said.

"Of course, he's gonna have kids. Deke's gotta score someplace," their star forward replied. A few more salacious words were uttered before the men made their way to the locker room. As Harry was about to join them, the doors opened, and twenty teenage boys hit the ice. They skated a circle, then stopped in front of Harry.

"Look! It's Deke Edwards!" said one dark-haired boy, pointing.

They stopped in front of Harry.

"Are you really Deke Edwards?" A blond boy asked.

"I am."

"Are you going to coach us?"

"Yeah. Of course, he is. Why else would he be here?"

"Really?"

"I saw you in the playoffs against Montreal."

"Me, too. On TV."

"You saved the game."

"Yeah. You kept them from scoring."

"That last shot. Wow."

"How'd you know he was gonna shoot?"

"Well, boys. It was like this..." Harry began.

The teens gathered around. Some stood by the railing, others filled the seats next to Harry. Words flowed like a good day on the ice.

Harry shot a look at Kitty. Sure enough, she blushed. She'd been part of this ambush. Probably her, Timmons, and that Buster guy. Three against one—he'd been seriously outnumbered. He wove his tale of hockey excellence, painting himself the hero. Damn, he deserved to be the hero, because he'd defended their lead and played a key role in winning the game.

"Okay, boys. Let's see what you can do," Harry said, rising to his feet. Glancing up, a puck appeared, as if by magic.

"Go on now. Half forwards, half defensemen. Go out there and try to score."

"So, you are going to be our coach?" a tall boy asked.

"Guess so. Can't let you all down now, can I?"

"No, sir."

The boys looked like a mishmash, all skating in opposite directions, trying to steal the puck, falling down, hitting the boards. They were committing a hundred fouls and infractions. Harry clucked to himself. What a disorganized bunch of hooligans who didn't know one end of a hockey stick from another. He shook his head. Turning these novices into hockey players would be a challenge. They'd need a firm hand, someone who knew hockey inside and out. How could he turn them down?

ONCE INSIDE HIS HOME, Harry went into the living room to start a fire. It was five already and their movie marathon awaited. He started the logs and then joined his wife in the kitchen.

"Turkey sandwiches are ready," she said, wiping her hands on her apron.

Harry pulled her into his embrace for a long, passionate kiss. When they broke, he spoke.

"You did that, didn't you?"

"Did what?"

"Arranged to have those boys there."

"I might have had something to do with it."

"I'm the luckiest man alive," he said, taking her hand and leading her over to the sofa. "Now about making babies..."

****THE END****

AUTHOR'S NOTE

F*inal Slapshot* was inspired by the true story of Trent McCleary, a professional hockey player whose career was ended by a slapshot to the throat. Read more about him on Wikipedia here: https://en.wikipedia.org/wiki/Trent_McCleary

Books by Jean C. Joachim

ECHOES OF THE HEART

HEATHER & MIKE: THE ONE THAT GOT AWAY

SANDY & RAFE: SECOND PLACE HEART

LIZ & NICK: NO REGRETS

PAIGE & BILL: ONE FINE DAY

ANTHOLOGY

BOTTOM OF THE NINTH

DAN ALEXANDER, PITCHER

MATT JACKSON, CATCHER

JAKE LAWRENCE, THIRD BASEMAN

NAT OWEN, FIRST BASE

BOBBY HERNANDEZ, SECOND BASE

SKIP QUINCY, SHORT STOP

EXTRA INNINGS

FIRST & TEN SERIES

GRIFF MONTGOMERY, QUARTERBACK

BUDDY CARRUTHERS, WIDE RECEIVER

PETE SEBASTIAN, COACH

DEVON DRAKE, CORNERBACK

SLY "BULLHORN" BRODSKY, OFFENSIVE LINE

AL "TRUNK" MAHONEY, DEFENSIVE LINE

HARLEY BRENNAN, RUNNING BACK
OVERTIME, THE FINAL TOUCHDOWN
A KING'S CHRISTMAS

THE MANHATTAN DINNER CLUB

RESCUE MY HEART
SEDUCING HIS HEART
SHINE YOUR LOVE ON ME
TO LOVE OR NOT TO LOVE

HOLLYWOOD HEARTS SERIES

IF I LOVED YOU
RED CARPET ROMANCE
MEMORIES OF LOVE
MOVIE LOVERS
LOVE'S LAST CHANCE
LOVERS & LIARS
His Leading Lady (Series Starter)

NOW AND FOREVER SERIES

NOW AND FOREVER 1, A LOVE STORY
NOW AND FOREVER 2, THE BOOK OF DANNY
NOW AND FOREVER 3, BLIND LOVE
NOW AND FOREVER 4, THE RENOVATED HEART
NOW AND FOREVER 5, LOVE'S JOURNEY
NOW AND FOREVER, CALLIE'S STORY (prequel)

MOONLIGHT SERIES

SUNNY DAYS, MOONLIT NIGHTS
APRIL'S KISS IN THE MOONLIGHT
UNDER THE MIDNIGHT MOON
MOONLIGHT & ROSES (prequel)

LOST & FOUND SERIES

LOVE, LOST AND FOUND

DANGEROUS LOVE, LOST AND FOUND

NEW YORK NIGHTS NOVELS

THE MARRIAGE LIST

THE LOVE LIST

THE DATING LIST

PINE GROVE SERIES

UNPREDICTABLE LOVE

BREAK MY HEART

RENOVATING THE BILLIONAIRE

SHORT STORIES

SWEET LOVE REMEMBERED

TUFFER'S CHRISTMAS WISH

THE HOUSE-SITTER'S CHRISTMAS

About the Author

Jean Joachim is an award-winning, international, USA Today best-selling romance fiction author, with books hitting the Amazon Top 100 list since 2012. She writes contemporary romance, which includes sports romance and romantic suspense.

Liz & Nick: One Fine Day won second place in the erotic romance category of the Oklahoma Romance Writers of America's International Digital Awards.

Dangerous Love Lost & Found, First Place winner in the 2015 Oklahoma Romance Writers of America, International Digital Award contest. *The Renovated Heart* won Best Novel of the Year from Love Romances Café. *Lovers & Liars* was a RomCon finalist in 2013. And *The Marriage List* tied for third place as Best Contemporary Romance from the Gulf Coast RWA.

To Love or Not to Love tied for second place in the 2014 New England Chapter of Romance Writers of America Reader's Choice contest.

She was chosen Author of the Year in 2012 by the New York City chapter of RWA.

Married and the mother of two sons, Jean lives in New York City. Early in the morning, you'll find her at her computer, writing, with a cup of tea, and a secret stash of black licorice.

Jean has 48 books, novellas and short stories published. Find it here: http://www.jeanjoachimbooks.com. Chat with Jean in her Facebook group, JJ's Book Buddies. Join here: https://www.facebook.com/groups/489790604419710/

www.ingramcontent.com/pod-product-compliance
Lightning Source LLC
Chambersburg PA
CBHW070450170726
48291CB00005B/1686

* 9 7 8 1 9 4 5 3 6 0 0 5 3 *